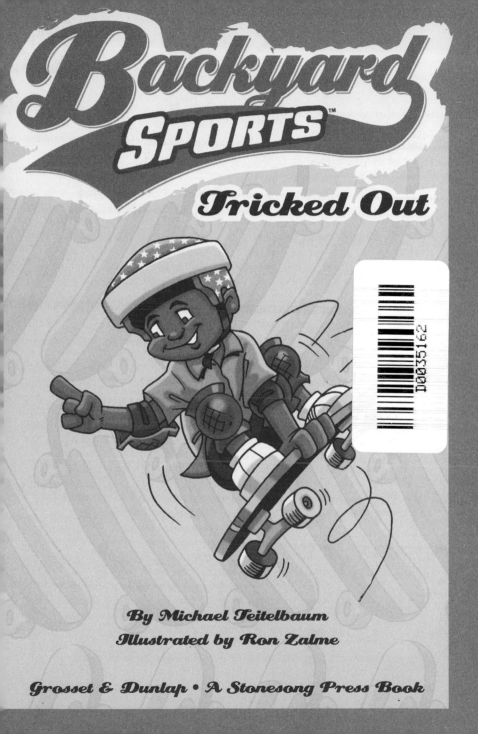

Backyard SPORTS™

Tricked Out

By Michael Teitelbaum

Illustrated by Ron Zalme

Grosset & Dunlap • A Stonesong Press Book

A Stonesong Press Book

GROSSET & DUNLAP
Published by the Penguin Group
Penguin Group (USA) Inc., 375 Hudson Street, New York, New York 10014, USA
Penguin Group (Canada), 90 Eglinton Avenue East, Suite 700,
Toronto, Ontario M4P 2Y3, Canada
(a division of Pearson Penguin Canada Inc.)
Penguin Books Ltd., 80 Strand, London WC2R 0RL, England
Penguin Group Ireland, 25 St. Stephen's Green, Dublin 2, Ireland
(a division of Penguin Books Ltd.)
Penguin Group (Australia), 250 Camberwell Road, Camberwell,
Victoria 3124, Australia
(a division of Pearson Australia Group Pty. Ltd.)
Penguin Books India Pvt. Ltd., 11 Community Centre, Panchsheel Park,
New Delhi—110 017, India
Penguin Group (NZ), 67 Apollo Drive, Rosedale, North Shore 0632,
New Zealand (a division of Pearson New Zealand Ltd.)
Penguin Books (South Africa) (Pty.) Ltd., 24 Sturdee Avenue,
Rosebank, Johannesburg 2196, South Africa

Penguin Books Ltd., Registered Offices: 80 Strand, London WC2R 0RL, England

Library of Congress Cataloging-in-Publication Data is available.

ISBN 978-0-448-45072-8   10 9 8 7 6 5 4 3 2 1

Chapter One

"Hey, guys, check out this move!" Dante Robinson shouted as he zoomed across the playground on his skateboard. Dante and his friends Reese Worthington, Ernie Steele, Vicki Kawaguchi, and Joey MacAdoo were hanging out on the playground practicing their skateboarding.

Keeping his left foot firmly planted on the skateboard, Dante pushed off with his right foot, picking up speed. He was headed for a curved ramp known as a quarter-pipe. The quarter-pipe ramp started at ground level, then curved up to a flat platform at the top.

Dante hit the bottom of the quarter-pipe

at top speed. He glided smoothly up the
ramp. Reaching the top of the ramp, Dante
waited until the two front wheels of his
skateboard went over the edge of the
platform. Shifting his weight to his back
foot, he spun on the back wheels until he
was facing the bottom of the ramp. Then he
skated back down. A smile spread across his
face. Nothing gave him more satisfaction

than pulling off a perfect skateboarding move.

"Wicked frontside 180, Dante!" his best friend Reese shouted. The frontside 180 was a move they had both been practicing.

"Wow!" Ernie added. "I'm happy when I can just make it up the quarter-pipe without falling off. You got the moves of a pro, Dante."

"It's just practice, guys," Dante said sheepishly. "Practice, practice, practice."

"Ugh. I hate practicing!" Ernie groaned. "I'd rather just be as good as you, naturally."

Dante laughed. "Even *I'm* not as good as me naturally!"

Dante was the best skateboarder in the group. He'd been skating longer than any of his friends, and he loved helping them improve their skills. "Show 'em what you've got, Reese," Dante suggested.

Reese tossed his skateboard out in front

of him. He took two steps forward and jumped onto the moving board. After Dante, Reese was the best skateboarder among his friends. The two of them spent hours skating together, even when their friends were off playing other sports. But today no one was focused on anything except skating.

Reese approached a barrel that the group had set up on the playground.

"Watch Reese. He's gonna pop an ollie!" Joey said excitedly.

"He's gonna pop an ollie?" Ernie asked. "Why can't he pop an Ernie?"

"Just watch and learn, Ernie," Vicki said. "An ollie is a classic skateboard move."

"I knew that," Ernie said quickly.

Just as Reese reached the barrel, he bent his knees. Then he stepped down hard on the back end of his board. As the front of his board started to rise, Reese jumped up.

His skateboard popped into the air. Reese

sailed over the barrel and landed on the other side, then skated smoothly back over to the group.

"Whoo-hoo!" Reese shouted, pumping his fist. "No hands, all air!"

"In other words, you popped an ollie," Ernie said casually.

"Try one, Ernie," Dante said. "Go ahead."

"Sure," Ernie replied. He jumped onto his skateboard and crouched. "Hey, someone took the engine out of this thing. It's not moving!"

Dante laughed at Ernie's goofy joke. "That board runs on Ernie power."

Ernie pushed off with his right foot and picked up speed.

"Just try the ollie on flat ground," Dante suggested. "They'll be plenty of time to jump barrels once you get the move down."

Ernie sped along the playground's blacktop.

"Remember," Dante said, "stay crouched. Kick down on the back of the board, then jump up. Try to keep your feet on the board at all times."

Ernie's face was intent with concentration.

Vicki began to giggle.

"What's so funny?" Joey asked.

"I've never seen Ernie look so serious," Vicki said, trying to stop laughing.

"Hey, that's a lot to remember. And there's a lot at stake here," Ernie shouted back, slowing down. "Like keeping all my bones in one piece. I like my bones that way."

"Focus, Ernie," Dante called out. "And get your speed back up."

Again Ernie pushed off and built up speed. He liked the thrill of skating, but he was always a little nervous trying tricks. He really wanted to be a good skateboarder.

He just wasn't crazy about the falling down part.

Ernie crouched, then stepped down hard on the back of his board. He jumped straight up. His skateboard shot out from under him and flew into the air, landing about ten feet away.

"Well, your board did an ollie," said Vicki, who was never able to resist giving Ernie a hard time. "Too bad you didn't stick around for the ride."

"Maybe I should've glued my feet to the board," Ernie said as he chased down his skateboard. As usual, he was trying to cover his disappointment with a joke.

"You've got to shift your weight forward as you make the jump," Reese explained. "That way you stick with the board. Try it again."

Ernie once again built up his speed. This time he popped into the air and shifted his weight toward the front of the board. He stayed on top of it, but when he landed, the board hit the ground and spun out from under him. Ernie stumbled but kept his footing. The board tumbled end over end and rolled to a stop.

"Better!" Dante said. "You just have to land with your feet in the center of the board."

"There are too many things to remember," Ernie said, picking up his board in frustration. "Maybe I should make a checklist."

"Nope," Dante shook his head. "A checklist isn't going to do it. The only thing that will help you is—"

"I know," Ernie said, sighing. "Practice, practice, practice."

"Why don't you try something, Joey," Dante suggested.

"Sure," Joey replied, dropping his

skateboard and jumping on. "But I'm going to do something a little closer to the ground."

"Like falling?" Ernie joked.

"Not if I do it right," Joey shot back, slipping on a pair of batting gloves he used when he played baseball. "I'm gonna try a Bert Slide."

Joey pushed off with his left foot a few times. When he had gained enough speed, he crouched down very close to the ground. Slowing down slightly, he leaned back even farther and planted his left hand on the

ground. Using his hand as a pivot, Joey circled around it until he was facing back in the direction he had started. The batting glove protected his hand. Standing up, he hopped off his skateboard and raised his hands triumphantly.

"You rule, Joey!" Reese shouted, hopping onto his skateboard and whipping around low to the ground, doing his own Bert Slide. Joey's slide had been good, but Reese's slide looked effortless.

"How do you make it look so easy, Reese?" Joey asked, stomping on the back of his skateboard and flipping it up into his hands.

"It gets easier every time you do it," Reese said. "I mean, Dante has practiced more and his looks even better than mine."

"You try one, Vicki," Dante said.

"Yeah, Vicki, show us how it's done," Ernie said.

"How what's done, Ernie?" Vicki replied.

"Actually staying on my board?"

"That would be good, yeah," Ernie said.

"I'm stoked to try the quarter-pipe," Vicki said, stepping onto her board.

"Go for it," Dante said. "Just make sure you've got enough speed when you hit the ramp to make it all the way up to the top."

With one foot on her board, Vicki pushed off the ground with her other foot. She streaked along the blacktop heading for the quarter-pipe. When she hit the bottom of the ramp, she crouched.

"Lean forward!" Dante shouted.

Vicki leaned forward as she approached the top of the ramp. She hadn't quite made it all the way up when she ran out of momentum. Her skateboard slowed down.

"It's okay, Vicki!" Dante called out. "Just look back this way and slide on down."

Vicki turned her head so she was now facing the bottom of the ramp. Her board

11

began rolling back down. She slid off the bottom of the ramp and slowed to a stop.

"Awesome!" Ernie cried.

"Really?" Vicki asked hopefully as she stepped off her board.

"Nah," Ernie replied. "I just thought it was a cool thing to say."

"It *was* awesome, Vicki," Dante said. "You kept your control and stayed on the board all the way through the move. That's what counts. You'll be doing flips and turns soon enough."

"Show us one, Dante," Joey asked.

Dante nodded, then tossed his board out in front of him. Jumping on, he sped toward the quarter-pipe. He glided up the curve. Reaching the top, his board kept going, soaring above the ramp. He grabbed the board in midair with his hand, spun around, and landed back on the ramp for the ride down.

"Nice aerial, Dante!" shouted Pablo Sanchez, another one of their friends, from across the playground. He had just arrived at the park with his skateboard in one  hand and a newspaper clipping in the other.

"Hey, Pablo, what've you got?" Reese asked.

"They just announced this year's big skateboard tournament," Pablo explained. "It starts in two weeks. And first prize is a brand-new, tricked out, top-of-the-line *Airborne 4000* skateboard!"

"The *Airborne 4000!*" Reese shouted, jumping off his board and grabbing the clipping out of Pablo's hand. "That baby's got a wicked 8x32-inch deck, with jet plane graphics, and clear blue wheels. It's like riding a cloud!"

"How do you know all that?" Vicki asked.

"Are you kidding?" Reese replied. "It's the cover story in this month's *Skate World Magazine*! I put the picture up in my room!"

"That *is* one sweet board," Dante admitted. He imagined himself gliding up the quarter-pipe on the *Airborne 4000*, doing trick after outrageous trick.

"So why don't you go win it?" Ernie cried. "You and Reese should enter this year! You've gotten really good."

The tournament was a local annual tradition. None of the friends ever felt that they were even close to being good enough to enter, but Dante and Reese were much better now than they'd ever been before.

"Wicked idea, Ernie!" Reese shouted. He jumped onto his board, sped up the half-pipe, and rode along the ramp's top edge before smoothly gliding back down. "We're gonna go to the tournament. And I'm gonna win that skateboard. Whoo!"

Dante looked away. "I don't know, Reese," he said reluctantly.

"Don't worry, dude," Reese said. "I'll let you have a ride on my new board."

"It's not that, Reese," Dante said.

"Then what's the problem?" Reese asked, slightly annoyed that Dante wasn't as flat-out excited as he was.

"Yeah," Joey said. "What's the problem? You're the best skateboarder we know."

Everyone stared at Dante, waiting for his answer.

Chapter Two

"The problem," Dante began, "is that I may be the best skateboarder all of you know, but I'm far from the best skateboarder around here."

"Come on, Dante," Ernie said. "You rule!"

Dante shook his head, a little annoyed that his friends didn't understand his hesitation. "The guys who enter this tournament are way good. I mean, wicked good."

Reese was growing impatient with his best friend. "We should just go for it, Dante." Reese hopped onto his board and gathered up some speed. Then he jumped into the air. His feet left the board, which spun completely around in the air beneath him in a perfect kickflip. He landed on the board just as it returned to the ground. "What have we got to lose?"

Dante thought for a moment. Then he jumped on his board and pushed off. *Maybe Reese is right*, he thought. *It might be fun to compete even if we don't win.* He leaped up, and his board came with him. He spun through the air in a complete circle, his feet never leaving the board; then he landed his 360 flip.

"Okay," he said as Reese gave him a high five. "I'm in!"

"With moves like that, how could you lose?" Ernie asked, jumping onto his board and attempting to copy Dante's move. Ernie leaped into the air. His board went in one direction and Ernie went in another, landing on his butt.

"So let me take a wild guess here, Ernie," Vicki said, helping Ernie up. "You won't be entering the contest."

"Not likely," Ernie replied. "But I will be there to root these guys on."

"We all will!" Joey said.

Reese was starting to get really excited. "This is going to be very cool!"

"There's just one thing," Dante said seriously. "If we're going to enter this contest and not embarrass ourselves, we're going to have to bring our skating up to the next level. And you know what that means, Reese."

Reese didn't reply. He was too busy picturing himself riding his brand-new *Airborne 4000*.

"Um, what does it mean, Dante?" Vicki asked, staring at her friend.

"As much fun as it is to hang out and skateboard with you guys, this is still just a playground," Dante explained. "If we're going to be good enough to compete, we'll have to start training at the real skateboarding park. They've got a huge half-pipe. It's like two quarter-pipes stuck together. You can ride the ramp back and forth all day just using gravity. And they have a big bowl where you can do some wicked aerial maneuvers. Plus you can add as many as four barrels to jump over."

"Gee, it sounds like a real nightmare for someone who loves to skateboard," Vicki said sarcastically, looking at Dante.

"It's not the equipment that's the problem," Dante told her "It's the kids who hang out there. It's a tough crowd. They're all really good, and they take skateboarding way more seriously than we do. In fact, they take everything way more seriously. They're not exactly a fun bunch."

"So we don't make any new friends," Reese said, skating up beside Dante. "Big deal. We're just there to improve our skateboarding moves. It'll be cool. Don't worry so much."

"Those guys can be really nasty," Dante reminded Reese. "Especially to newcomers. You and I have watched them at the park, but we've always been too scared to go in with our boards, remember?"

Reese thought about this for a second, then tossed his board out in front of him and jumped on. "Hey, I'm ready to do whatever it takes to win the coolest skateboard on Earth!" he said. Then he launched himself over the barrel, landed, spun around in a frontside 180, and jumped back over the barrel.

Dante shrugged and jumped onto his board. *Maybe Reese is right*, he thought. *Maybe it'll be okay after all.*

He sped toward the quarter-pipe at full speed, zoomed up to the top, and then twisted with his back wheel on the top edge of the ramp. "I guess I am a little stoked," he admitted as he skated out of the quarter-pipe.

"Way to grind and pivot, Dante!" Reese shouted. "We'll show those tough guys a few things."

"I could show them how to fall on their butts," Ernie joked. "But they probably learned how to do that a long time ago."

"You guys are going to the tournament!" Joey shouted, giving Dante and Reese high fives as they rolled past on their boards.

"Yeah, and no loser tough guys are gonna stop you," Vicki added. "Or they'll have to answer to Ernie."

"Right!" Ernie agreed. "They'll have to answer to—huh? What did you just say?"

Chapter Three

The next day, Dante and Reese showed up at the skateboarding park. By the time they arrived, a crowd of kids was already there working on their moves.

"Look at this place," Reese said, getting excited thinking about using the amazing ramps and other equipment. He stared at the skateboarders who were zooming around doing high-level moves. "This place is so cool."

"We can definitely get a lot better practicing here," Dante agreed. "Come on. Let's just go watch for a while and check it out."

The two friends took a spot next to the half-pipe ramp. The curved ramp was high on both sides and low in the middle. The ramp curved smoothly so that a skater could use momentum to roll back and forth. A level platform extended out from the highest point on each end. This was where the skateboarders started. They dropped into the curve from one of the platforms and let gravity and their own skills do the rest.

As Dante and Reese looked on, a skater was right in the middle of zooming back and forth on the half-pipe. Each time he reached the top of the ramp, he did another complicated trick. He sent three of his four wheels above the lip of the platform, then pivoted on the fourth wheel and shot back down the ramp.

"Go for some air!" shouted one of the kids who was watching. He was the biggest kid in the park by far. He had a mop of bright red hair and a scary-looking scowl spread across his face.

"That's Chuck," Dante whispered, pointing at the kid who had just yelled. "He won the tournament last year."

The skater on the ramp reached the low point of the half-pipe, then started his run up the other side. At the top of the ramp, he tried to lift his board completely above the platform. But he couldn't get up high enough and had to settle for a quick turn.

"What's your problem, Freddie?" Chuck shouted as the skater slid back down, then jumped off the ramp. "My grandmother could make that move with her eyes closed."

"Hey, Freddie. Maybe you should give your board to Chuck's grandmother!" shouted a short kid who stood on the side holding his own board.

The others in the park cracked up and pointed at Freddie, who walked away shaking his head. Then he stopped and turned back to face Chuck, the anger clear on his face.

"Who are you to talk?" Freddie yelled back to the short kid. "I've never seen you do an aerial, big shot!"

"Why do they have to be so nasty to each other?" Reese whispered, starting to feel a little nervous about skating in front of these guys. "I mean Ernie and Vicki are always giving each other a hard time, but they're just kidding around."

"It's a whole different world here," Dante replied anxiously. He knew all along how tough the kids in this park were. He realized that Reese was just starting to understand what they were about to deal with.

"Let me show you guys how it's done," Chuck boasted, snatching up his board and heading toward a deep pit known as the bowl. The bowl looked like a big, empty,

round swimming pool, but it was designed
for skating.

Chuck dropped in from the edge. He
squatted as he sped down toward the
bottom. Reaching the lowest point in the
bowl, he zoomed up the opposite side, then
weaved up and down as he raced along the
side of the bowl.

"He looks like a surfer riding a wave!"
Reese exclaimed, amazed by Chuck's fluid

moves as he rode down and cut back up the side of the bowl. Reese wondered if he would be able to pull off that move.

"That's the whole idea," Dante said. "The best skateboarders make it look like they're surfing on cement."

Turning with a sharp frontside 180 near the top edge of the bowl, Chuck rolled down to the bottom again. This time he kept going. Up he went, speeding up the opposite side.

"Now this is how it's done, boys," Chuck shouted as he approached the far edge of the bowl. "Watch the master and learn."

Chuck reached the top of the bowl and just kept going. His board flew above the edge until it was completely in the air. He grabbed the center of his board with his hand. Then he spun around in a complete 360 before landing back on the wall and sliding down.

"Now that, you bunch of losers, is an aerial," Chuck announced. He sped up the wall of the bowl, then stepped out when he reached the top.

"He's really good," Reese said nervously as it began to dawn on him just how talented the competition was going to be. "We're going to have to go up against him in the tournament, right?"

"Yup," Dante said, taking a deep breath. He noticed a bunch of kids dropping into the bowl all at the same time. Skaters zoomed up and down, pulling off turns and jumps. "We've got to jump in sometime, Reese. This looks like a good time. With all those kids in the bowl at the same time, maybe no one will notice us. Come on."

The two friends grabbed their boards and hurried over to the bowl. When two skaters pulled out of the bowl, Dante and Reese dropped in.

"Hey, who are you?" Chuck shouted as soon as Dante and Reese had entered the bowl.

"Just a couple of guys who like to skateboard, like you," Dante said, trying to sound as casual as he could. He glided up the side of the bowl, whipped his board around, and sped back down.

"Nobody skates like me. Maybe you guys are in the wrong place," Chuck said. "The park for babies is just up the road."

Dante just shrugged and kept skating.

The rest of the skateboarders howled with laughter.

"Hey, this park is open to anyone!" Reese shouted, less able to keep his cool.

"Really?" Chuck shot back. "Well, what time is your mommy picking you up?"

Again the others burst into laughter.

"What a jerk," Reese mumbled.

"Forget it," Dante said as he and Reese

rode up and out of the bowl. "Just focus on
your skating. Ignore those guys."

The friends headed for the barrels next.
Two barrels were lined up. One by one,
skateboarders sped toward them. Just
before reaching the first barrel, the skaters

popped their boards into the air. They sailed over the two barrels, landing cleanly on the other side in a crouch.

Dante and Reese got into line.

"I've never jumped over two barrels, Dante," Reese whispered anxiously. "We only have one in our playground. I don't want to mess up in front of these guys."

"Piece of cake, Reese," Dante said. "Just pull your knees up a little higher when you go into the jump, and you'll get all the air you need. Watch these guys."

Dante stood ready as the skater in front of him took off and leaped over the barrels. Now it was his turn.

Dante dropped his skateboard and stepped onto it with his left foot. He pushed off hard with his right foot, once, twice, three times. Then he settled both feet onto the board, shifted his weight, and set himself up to do an ollie.

Just before he reached the barrels, he squatted slightly. Then he slammed down onto the back of his board with his back foot while jumping as high as he could with his front foot. With his feet still pressed against his board, Dante sailed up and over the two barrels. He landed cleanly on the wheels, knees bent, arms outstretched.

"Good one, Dante!" Reese shouted, still wondering if he would be able to clear two barrels.

"Oh yeah, 'good one,'" Chuck repeated in a mocking tone. "Two barrels. Wow! Somebody should call the newspaper. Or maybe you should even sign up for the tournament if you're good enough to jump over two whole barrels."

"We *are* going to the tournament!" Reese shouted, annoyed that Chuck had made fun of Dante's perfectly executed jump.

"There's no junior division in the

tournament, dweeb," Chuck said. "Serious skateboarders only."

"Oh, yeah," Reese shot back. "What are you going to be doing that day?"

"Oooh!" Chuck's friends all groaned, looking at one another, wondering how Chuck would handle this newcomer.

"I'm gonna be kicking your butt that day, dweeb," Chuck replied. "And winning the tournament just like I did last year."

"His name's Reese," Dante said, returning to the line.

"That's what I said, 'dweeb,'" Chuck joked, looking back at all his friends. "You're up, dweeb. Don't hold up the line for the real skateboarders."

Reese jumped onto his board and pushed off hard. He sped toward the barrels, still upset by Chuck's taunting. *Stay focused*, he said to himself. *You don't want to mess up in front of these guys.*

Reaching the barrels, Reese popped into the air and easily cleared them both. He landed cleanly, then spun a frontside 180 and hopped off his board.

"Ooh, I'm scared," Chuck said sarcastically. "Maybe I should drop out of the tournament. These guys are just too good. What do you think, Steve?"

"Maybe none of us should go to the tournament," Chuck's friend Steve said. "Oh, wait. I have an idea. See if these chumps can pull off a Bert inside the bowl."

"Good idea, Steve," Chuck said, jumping onto his skateboard and rolling over to the bowl. He stopped at the edge, turned back, and looked right at Dante and Reese. "Okay, try this."

Chuck dropped into the bowl. He zoomed down one side, then up the other. As he approached the top of the bowl, he leaned his body backward and touched the wall with his hand. Then he spun his board in a complete circle, pivoting around his hand. His feet stayed planted on his board. His movement was smooth and fluid. Then he stood back up, and skated across the bottom of the bowl and up the other side. He stepped out and popped his board up into his hands.

Without hesitation Dante stepped up to the edge of the bowl. "Oh, you mean like this," he said. Dante dropped into the bowl. Following Chuck's moves exactly, he skated down the side of the bowl, across the bottom, and back up the other side. Near the top of the bowl, he dropped his hand down behind him and spun around, completing a perfect Bert. Then he raced back across the bowl and popped out at the same spot where he had dropped in.

Chuck sneered and looked away. "Yeah, yeah, big deal," he said, obviously annoyed. "So you can do a Bert. Whoopee."

Reese stepped up to the edge of the bowl. He was quickly realizing that the only way to earn the respect of these skateboarders was to show that he wasn't afraid of them— and to show that he was as good as they were.

He dropped into the bowl, sped across the bottom, and rose up the other side. Just before he reached the edge, Reese dropped backward, planted his hand, and started his spin. But his board slipped out from under his feet and tumbled down to the bottom of the bowl. Reese followed, rolling down the steep wall and landing at the bottom.

Dante jumped back onto his board and sped down to the bottom of the bowl. "Are you all right?" he asked, jumping off his board. He helped Reese back to his feet.

"I'm fine!" Reese shouted angrily, annoyed at himself. Looking up, he saw Chuck pointing down at him.

"Nice move, dweeb!" Chuck said, laughing. "What do you call that one? It's more like a 'Butt' than a 'Bert'!"

The other skaters lining the edge all laughed and stared down at Reese and Dante.

"Dante," Reese said through clenched teeth. "We have got to go to the tournament and beat this guy!"

Chapter Four

For the next week, Dante and Reese got to the skateboard park early every day. This allowed them to get in a few solid hours of practice before Chuck and his friends showed up—which meant they could work on more difficult moves without worrying about Chuck's put-downs. They had been focusing on skateboarding all day, every day, but they were both still pretty stressed out about mastering as many new tricks as they could before the competition.

"Let's just warm up in the half-pipe for a bit," Dante said to Reese as he dropped in from the top platform.

"It's cool being here before anybody else," Reese said, joining Dante on the ramp. "That way we don't have to deal with that jerk. All I have to think about are my moves. Today, I want to try a 360 aerial, and I'm going for three barrels."

"I want to practice adding a backside 180 to my jump over the barrels," Dante said. "If I can turn halfway around in midair and still clear the barrels, it'll take the jump to the next level."

Dante went back and forth from one side of the half-pipe to the other. At the top point of each side, he did a smooth frontside 180. Then he headed back down in the other direction. Once he felt he was warmed up, he began skating faster and faster.

"Check this out," Dante said, zooming down one side and racing up the other. He reached the top of the ramp and just kept going up into the air. When his skateboard

was no longer
touching the
ramp, Dante
grabbed his
board and
spun himself around
completely. Finishing
the 360 aerial, he landed
back on the ramp and slid
down triumphantly.

"Let me try," Reese said quickly. He stood
at the platform at the top of the half-pipe.

Dropping into the ramp, he slid from side
to side. On his third trip up, he kept going.
Reese's board cleared the top of the ramp.
He grabbed it with his hand. But when
he tried to spin, he only made it halfway
around.

Reese hit the ramp facing backward and
slid back down. "I missed it!" he shouted
in frustration, hopping off the half-pipe.

"I've got to get that move down if I'm going to beat Chuck. And I really want to beat Chuck! Maybe even more than you do. I'm the one he laughed at. I'm the one he calls 'dweeb.'"

"Stay cool, Reese," Dante said. He couldn't remember ever seeing his friend so upset. "You just need to get a little higher, so you're in the air long enough to complete this spin."

"You mean, like you?" Reese asked sharply.

"Um, yeah, I guess," Dante said hesitantly. *What's he snapping at me for? Maybe he just needs to take a break and come back to this trick later*, Dante thought. "I think we should take a break from the half-pipe. Let's work on our barrel jumps." Then he skated over to the barrels.

Two barrels were lined up. Dante pushed off and picked up speed. He knew he could jump straight over two barrels with no problem. But this time, he wanted to add a backside 180 to the mix.

He started out with his left foot toward the front of the board. If he could pull off this move, he would turn backward, leading with his front shoulder, so that he was facing in the opposite direction when he landed. His right foot would end up in front.

"Watch this," Dante said. As he reached the first barrel, he popped into the air. Once he had left the ground, Dante spun back, leading with his left shoulder—but his feet stayed in contact with the skateboard.

As he cleared the second barrel, he completed his turn so that his right shoulder was now in front. Then he landed smoothly and glided to a stop.

"Your turn," he called back to Reese.

Reese skated over to the barrels without saying a word. He had jumped two barrels before, and he had pulled off a backside 180 on level ground. But he had never combined the two moves as Dante had just done.

Why do I feel so nervous? Reese wondered. *I'm just doing this in front of Dante. It's not like Chuck is here or anything.*

Trying to shrug off his nerves, Reese gathered speed. He popped an ollie and lifted above the first barrel. Then he spun backward as he began coming down. Just barely clearing the second barrel, Reese's skateboard hit the ground unevenly. The board wobbled, forcing Reese to step off. He was furious.

"I blew it!" Reese shouted. "I'm going again."

Skating back around to the first barrel, Reese took off again, faster this time. He launched himself into the air and spun with such force that he whipped around in a complete 360 degree circle, landing facing the same direction he had started in. This time he stayed on his board.

"Yeah!" Reese shouted, pumping his right fist in the air. "Beat that!" *Finally!* Reese thought. *I'm gonna prove to all of them, even Dante, that I can skate just as well as they can!*

'Beat that?' Dante thought, losing his temper. *That sounds like something Chuck would say. Well if that's the way he wants it, that's what he'll get.*

He grabbed a third barrel and added it to the end of the barrels. Then he snatched up his board and skated around to the front. He sped toward the barrels, then jumped, pulling his knees way up. Dante soared over all three barrels and landed cleanly on the other side.

"There," Dante said gruffly. "I just did!"

Reese slammed his board to the ground and jumped on. He had never attempted to jump over three barrels, but he was not going to let Dante show him up.

He raced toward the barrels and launched himself into the air. He cleared the first two barrels with no problem. Coming down, his board caught the third barrel and spun out from under him. He managed to land on his feet as his board tumbled and clattered to a stop.

"Well, that one needs some work," Dante said critically. Reese's challenges were starting to really get to him.

"I can see that!" Reese shouted, snatching his board off the ground angrily. "You know,

I want to win this contest as much as you do."

"Well you're going to have to get past me first," Dante said, losing his temper. Then he skated back around and repeated his jump over the three barrels.

On Reese's next try, he too cleared all three.

"Nice one, Reese!" Joey said as Reese landed the jump.

Reese spun around to see Ernie, Vicki, Joey, and Pablo walking into the park.

"I've only seen you clear one barrel on the playground," Joey continued. "And now you're up to three. Awesome!"

"I'm jumping three, also, you know!" Dante added quickly.

"Good," Ernie said. "Three is good. Between the two of you that's six."

"So how's it going?" Vicki asked, sensing the obvious tension in the air. "You guys seem a little stressed."

"No kidding!" Reese said. "The tournament is just a few days away. Dante is trying to show me up. What would I have to be stressed about?"

"Everything was fine until Reese started getting all bent out of shape," Dante explained.

"Me?" Reese cried. "You're the one who kept pushing me, adding barrels, challenging me to keep up."

"Well how are you gonna get better if you don't keep pushing?" Dante shot back. "Chuck and those other guys are not going to make it easy. So it's get better or go home!"

"Come on, guys," Pablo said, trying to smooth things out. "I thought you were in this together."

"Tell that to the champ here," Reese snarled, pointing at Dante.

"You guys are, like, best friends," Ernie

added. "You're a team. You go together like bacon and eggs, milk and cookies, fries and ketchup."

"What's with you and all the food?" Vicki asked Ernie.

"I'm hungry," he replied, rubbing his belly and laughing halfheartedly.

"Yeah, well this is *not* a team sport," Reese said firmly. "It's skater against skater, and the best skater wins."

"And that's gonna be me!" Dante announced, lining up to jump over three barrels again.

Dante and Reese continued to practice their jumps, adding turns and fancy moves. Their friends watched, but they weren't impressed with what they saw.

"I thought we'd come here and find them having a great time," Pablo said, shaking his head. "Now they're barely speaking to each other."

"I know they both want to win that skateboard, but I didn't think the tournament would mess up their friendship," Joey added. "Those two have been skating together since they each got their first boards."

"Maybe we should say something?" Ernie said. "You know, tell them to shake hands and make up and play nice."

Before anyone else could say a word, Reese hopped off his skateboard, grabbed another barrel, and added it to the line.

"Four barrels?" Dante shouted. "You're nuts. You're not really gonna try to jump four barrels, are you?"

"*You* may be afraid, but *I'm* not!" Reese yelled back.

"That's too many barrels," Joey said. "You just started doing three. Don't do it, Reese."

"I'm doing it!" Reese shouted, skating over to the front of the barrels.

Reese took a deep breath, then skated hard toward the barrels. He jumped, easily clearing the first three barrels. But he didn't have enough to make it over the last one. His board hit the fourth barrel, and Reese tumbled off, landing hard on the ground.

His friends all rushed over. Dante got to him first.

"Are you okay?" Dante asked, genuinely concerned.

"Yeah, I'm fine, leave me alone!" Reese cried, waving everyone away.

"No, you're not fine," Dante insisted. "Your elbow is cut; your leg is bruised. Come on, Reese, this has really gotten stupid. Look, I'm sorry I lost my temper. Let's stop competing against each other and work together again. I don't want to see you get hurt."

Dante extended a hand to help Reese up. Reese shoved Dante's hand aside, rolled

over, and stood up on his own. "You don't want to see me get hurt, huh? Why don't you just worry about you and leave me alone!" he shouted. "Because I'm going to win that tournament—and you're not going to stop me."

Reese stepped onto his board and skated away.

Dante was confused and frustrated. *How did things get so out of control?* he wondered. He was really hurt that Reese refused to make up with him.

"I tried," Dante said to his friends. "You saw it. He wouldn't even take my hand to help him up. I feel horrible. Reese has been putting a lot of pressure on both of us to beat Chuck, and I let it get to me. I shouldn't have tried to one-up him when he started challenging me. I want to make it better. I want it to be like it used to be, but I don't know how."

"It looks to me like Reese is not having fun skateboarding anymore," Joey said. "He's so caught up in win, win, win. Having fun is why he got into skateboarding in the first place."

"Well, well, well, what do we have here?" boomed a voice from the entrance to the park.

Dante turned around and saw Chuck and his friends arriving for their practice.

Oh great! Dante thought. *Just what we need.* "That's Chuck," he explained. "He and his buddies have been skating here for years."

"Hey, look guys," Chuck continued, pointing at Dante and his friends. "It's the geek squad here to watch their friends practice their little tricks."

"Who does this guy think he is?" Vicki said, scowling. "Does he think he owns the park or something?"

"Let me guess, Dante," Ernie said. "He's not your new best friend."

Chuck spotted Reese cleaning up his cuts and bruises.

"Oh, what's the matter?" Chuck asked. "Did dweeb get a boo-boo? Does he need his mommy to kiss it and make it better?"

Reese stared at Chuck, fuming. "Shut up, Chuck!" he shouted. "Just shut up."

"You gonna make me, dweeb?" Chuck

asked, stepping forward threateningly.

"I'm gonna do better than that," Reese said, jumping back onto his board. "I'm going to beat you in the tournament!"

Chuck and his buddies all cracked up.

Ernie looked at his friends, wondering just what Reese and Dante had gotten themselves into.

Chapter Five

When the day of the skateboarding
contest finally arrived, Reese still wasn't
talking to Dante. A local indoor arena had
been turned into a skateboard park for
the event. Two half-pipe ramps sat in the
center of the arena surrounded by seats for
spectators. The building was quickly filling
up with skateboarding fans.

Ernie, Vicki, Joey, and Pablo all showed
up to cheer for their friends.

"Look at this setup!" Joey said, his eyes
opening wide. "Brand-new half-pipes that
are as smooth as glass. They look like
they've never even been used."

"I hope Dante and Reese don't get too nervous skating in front of all these people," Pablo said.

"I hope they don't strangle each other before the tournament even begins," Vicki added. "They did not look happy at all when we left them at the skateboard park. They were not having any fun. And what is skateboarding if not full-throttle, pedal-to-the-metal fun?"

"Good point, Vicki," Joey said, starting to worry about his friends.

"There they are!" Pablo cried, pointing at Dante and Reese who had just entered the arena.

Down on the arena's floor, Dante and Reese mingled with the other skaters, but Reese was clearly trying to avoid Dante.

"Hey, good luck today," Dante said, walking over to Reese, hoping that maybe they could make up before the tournament

started. "I know you'll do a great job."

"Of course I will," Reese answered, turning away.

So much for making up, Dante thought.

"There's Chuck and Steve and a few of the other kids from the park," Dante said, trying again.

"I see them," Reese replied angrily. "But they can't bully anyone here. This is not their park. There are judges here to keep things fair and make sure that the best skater wins."

"Well then, I guess I should just take that *Airborne 4000* skateboard and go home right now," Dante said with a big smile, trying to joke with his friend. "Just kidding, buddy!"

"Yeah, well, this tournament is no joke," Reese snapped back. "I've been working just as hard as you. We still have to skate our runs to see who's better before you go home with that skateboard."

Dante searched his mind, trying to come up with something he could say that would calm his friend down. He was worried that Reese wouldn't skate his best if he was tense and angry. But before Dante could think of anything to say, the tournament director stepped up to the group of anxious skateboarders.

"Okay, competitors, listen up," he began. "We're going to form two lines, one behind each half-pipe. Two skaters will skate at the same time, one on each ramp. There are two sets of judges. Each set will score one of the skaters. Skaters with the highest scores in the early rounds will move on to the final rounds. May the best skater win!"

"He's talking about me, dweeb," Chuck whispered in Reese's ear.

Reese jumped back, startled. He hadn't noticed Chuck step up behind him while the director was speaking. But this time, Reese didn't reply; he just turned and walked over to the line.

Reese waited anxiously as skater after skater performed. When it was finally his turn, he climbed the steps up to the platform on one end of the half-pipe. The skaters began their routines from there, dropping down into the pipe, then returning to the starting platform when the run was over.

Reese heard his name announced over the loudspeakers. "Reese Worthington!"

"Whoo-hoo!" Ernie shouted, standing and applauding. "Go get 'em, Reese!"

Reese stood at the edge of the platform and thought about all the time and practice

he had put into this. Then he dropped in
and sped down the ramp.

Picking up speed, Reese zoomed up the
opposite side. When he was near the top
of the ramp, he spun back, doing a sharp
frontside 180, then glided down. At the top
of the other side, he put his hand on the
ramp, dropped his body down, and spun
around in a perfect Bert Slide.

Back and forth he went, pulling off move
after move. He
blocked out the
noise of the
cheering crowd
and thought of
nothing except
his next move.

When his
time was up,
Reese returned
to the starting

platform, brought his front wheels up over the lip, paused for a second, then leaned forward and came down neatly onto the platform.

"Great run, Reese!" Pablo shouted from his seat.

The judges agreed. Reese's score qualified him to move on to the next round.

As Reese left the platform, he passed Dante, who was skating next. "Beat that," Reese said, echoing the challenge he had given Dante in the park.

Dante just shook his head, trying to push his hurt feelings aside and focus on his run. Then he stepped onto his board.

"Dante Robinson!" boomed the voice through the loudspeakers.

"Go Dante!" Vicki shouted from the stands.

Dante slid into the half-pipe and immediately dropped into a crouch. As he hit the lowest point of the ramp, he popped straight up and kickflipped his board beneath him. The skateboard spun completely around and landed on its wheels. Dante's feet returned to the board, and he sped up the far side of the ramp.

Back and forth he rocked, cutting and turning at the top of each side of the ramp. He looked like he was surfing on the pavement. On his last trip up, Dante lifted above the lip of the far platform, grabbed his board, did a backside 180, and returned to the ramp. He slid down and back up to the starting platform, then stepped gently off the ramp.

"Oh, yeah!" Ernie cheered. "They are both doing great! Look, there's the judge's score. Dante's moved on to the next round, too!"

"Uh-oh," Vicki said, pointing up to the starting platform. "Look who's next!"

The friends looked up and saw Chuck

step onto the platform. His name was announced, and he dropped into the half-pipe.

"Wow!" Ernie exclaimed as Chuck tore through his moves. "He's good. Really good. He looks like he's moving at superspeed. Reese and Dante could be in trouble."

"It's a good thing you're not one of the judges then, isn't it?" Vicki said, scowling.

Chuck tore across the half-pipe as if his skateboard were jet-powered. Moving at blinding speed, he reached the top of the opposite ramp in no time. There, he pivoted on one wheel and whipped his board around, bringing it up over the edge of the far platform. Cruising down the ramp and back up the other side, he finished with a 360 aerial, spinning completely around. Then he landed back on the starting platform.

"You rule, Chuck!" his friends from the park shouted. "You're gonna win this competition again, just like last year."

Dante and Reese moved easily through the first rounds. As the competition tightened up, they both seemed to skate better with each run.

"Reese is doing the best skating of his life," Pablo said. "It's amazing how far he's come. Even if he's eliminated now, he should be happy with how well he skated."

"I don't know, Pabs," Ernie said. "I don't think he'll be happy unless he beats Chuck—and Dante."

The tournament moved into its final round. Four skaters remained—Dante, Reese, Chuck, and Steve, one of Chuck's friends from the park. One of the four skaters would win the grand prize and skate out of the arena on a brand-new board.

"Looks like you're gonna take home another first prize, Chuck," Steve said as the two waited for the finals to begin. "No one can beat you. Though that Dante kid's pretty good." Then Steve quickly looked around to see if Dante had heard him. He spotted Dante and Reese standing silently next to each other on the other side of the arena.

Chuck's score was way ahead of Steve's and Reese's. But Dante was only a few points behind him.

"Don't worry about Dante, Steve," Chuck replied, looking away. "He's not gonna be a problem."

In the first run of the finals, Chuck and Steve went head-to-head, one on each ramp. Both skated well, but it was obvious that Chuck had the better moves.

Chuck finished his run with a 360 aerial, soaring high above the starting platform. He landed on the platform, knees bent, arms spread wide. The crowd went wild.

Dante was waiting on the platform to

take his turn. His skateboard sat on the
platform beside him.

As Chuck brushed past him, heading for
the steps leading down off the platform, he
kicked Dante's board. The board tumbled off
of the platform and crashed onto the ground
below.

"Oh, I'm so sorry," Chuck said, mockingly. "Clumsy me."

"You did that on purpose!" Dante shouted.

"Prove it," Chuck whispered, smiling meanly. "Accidents happen, you know."

Dante dashed down the stairs and picked up his board. Reese, who had seen the whole thing, rushed over from the other half-pipe. He had been waiting to go head-to-head against Dante. Now he looked at his friend's skateboard in horror.

"My wheel is cracked!" Dante cried. "I can replace it at home, but that won't help me now!"

At that moment, the scores from the last ride were announced. Chuck had outscored Steve, eliminating him from the competition. Reese and Dante were the only two left to skate.

Then a voice came blasting from the

loudspeakers. "Reese Worthington, platform one. Dante Robinson, platform two."

"What am I going to do?" Dante cried. "If I can't go on now, I'll have to forfeit my turn!"

Chapter Six

Reese was furious. For the past few days, all he had thought about was beating Dante. He had lost track of the fact that Chuck was the one he really wanted to beat. It was Chuck who had called him names, Chuck who had put him down, and now it was Chuck who had cheated to knock his best friend out of the tournament.

Dante's been my best friend for as long as I can remember, Reese thought. *I can't believe I've been such a jerk to him about this contest. Our friendship is way more important than winning. Only one of us can skate, and I know who it has to be!*

"Here," Reese said, holding out his skateboard. "Take my board and go beat this guy!"

"But what about you?" Dante asked. "You won't get to skate."

"You've got a much better shot to beat Chuck," Reese said. "I'm sorry I've been such a jerk. I just really wanted to prove I was good enough, you know? But none of that really matters. You're my best friend, and I can't just watch you get knocked out of the tournament by a cheater."

Dante snatched the board from Reese's hands and slapped him on the back. "Apology accepted. You're the best, Reese. It's good to be on the same team again."

"Go get him!" Reese shouted. Then he headed over to the judge's table to explain that he would be giving up his turn and that Dante was using his board.

Dante bounded up the stairs and onto the platform. Glancing down, he saw Chuck standing below, scowling up at him. Chuck turned and walked away.

Dante took a deep breath. It was his turn to move so fast that he made all the other skaters, even Chuck, look as if they were skating in slow motion. He dropped into the half-pipe, whipped his board up the ramp, cut back sharply, and then tore down and back up the other side. He launched himself into aerial after aerial. The crowd went wild. He spun down into a Bert, then popped back up for yet another aerial, complete with a 360 spin.

Dante ended his run with a kickflip just before he reached the platform. The board spun completely around, then he caught it with his feet, and landed on all four wheels on the platform.

The cheering fans gave him a standing ovation. The judges gave him the highest score of any run that day—high enough to pass Chuck's total score. Dante had skated the best routine of his life and won the tournament.

Reese was waiting for Dante at the bottom of the stairs leading off the platform.

"I knew you could do it!" Reese cried, giving his friend a high five.

"I couldn't have done it without my best friend," Dante said, grinning broadly.

Ernie, Vicki, Pablo, and Joey rushed over and mobbed Dante.

"Awesome finish!" Ernie said. "I've never seen anyone do a kickflip coming up the ramp!"

"The whole run was awesome," Joey added.

"That Chuck is a real cheater," Vicki

said. "I saw what he did."

"That was nice of you to lend Dante your board, Reese," Pablo said.

"Hey, what are friends for?" Reese asked, smiling.

"Dante Robinson, please report to platform one!" came the announcement over the loudspeakers.

"Go get your prize," Reese said, patting Dante on the back.

Dante dashed up the stairs and onto the platform. The tournament director was standing there, holding a brand-new *Airborne 4000* skateboard.

"First place and the grand prize goes to Dante Robinson!" the director announced.

"Dante! Dante! Dante!" the crowd chanted.

Dante took the beautiful skateboard and held it over his head triumphantly.

"Dante! Dante! Dante!" the crowd

chanted again. Dante's friends were cheering the loudest.

Sprinting back down the stairs, Dante rejoined his friends.

"Do you need a pilot's license to operate that thing?" Ernie joked. "I hope it comes with a seat belt."

"Wow!" Pablo cried, staring at the board.

"It sure is beautiful," Joey said, spinning one of the wheels.

"I guess you won't need to fix your old one now, huh?" asked Reese.

"Actually, I *will* fix my old board," Dante said. "Because I'm giving this one to you."

He handed the skateboard to Reese.

"Are you kidding?" Reese asked, his eyes lighting up. "For real?"

"For real," Dante replied. "I couldn't have won it if you hadn't come through for me. Why don't you take the first run on it?"

"You bet!" Reese cried. Then he raced up

the stairs, placed the brand-new skateboard onto the platform, and dropped into the half-pipe.

"You rule, Dante!" Reese shouted as he streaked along on his brand-new skateboard.